SPRUCED UP

Spruced Up

A Maid in LA Mysteries

Holly Jacobs

Ilex Books 2018
ISBN-13: 978-0-9992736-7-8
ISBN-10: 0-9992736-7-1

This story is dedicated to everyone who's ever gone home for the holidays. Whether you're the friend who stayed in town, or the friend who left town—whenever friends get together, it's definitely a coming home. And on that note, this one's especially for Laurel, Mary Kay, and Betty Lou ... I always enjoy our homecoming get-togethers!

Thanks to everyone at *Erie Times-News* and *GoErie.com* who generously allowed me to add a fictional article about Quincy to their very real paper. The Erie Time-News is the paper that's waiting on my front porch every morning. I sit down and share my morning coffee with the Time's Public Editor, Liz Allen, and all her colleagues who work there.

And a special thanks to Jennifer Northrup for help with the doctor's office info. Any circumstances or information that was stretched is my fault!

Note from Holly: *I've heard from a lot of readers how much they enjoyed the 'reviews' in the first two Maid in LA Books. My family helped me with the ones for Steamed. My Duet friends showed their comedic roots by helping with reviews for Dusted. Since this is a Christmas novella, I knew just who to go to for 'reviews' for Spruced Up!*

REVIEWS:

"I fell in love with Quincy Mac when I learned she was once almost the spokeswoman for Dazzling Smile toothpaste. I have a fondness for great stories, for toothpaste… and for teeth." ~Hermey, Dentist to the North Pole

*"I'm jolly and happy to see you're setting this holiday novella in Erie, Pennsylvania. The words Lake Effect Snow are music to my family's ears—not that snowpeople have ears—and Erie weathermen and women use that term a lot. Oh, and **Spruced Up** is a fun story, too."* ~Frosty the Snowman

"I'm so glad to see your are finally making use of the typewriter I gave you when you were five. You've been so good this year, I think I'll bring you that Commodore 64 you've been asking for, Holly. Love that name." ~Santa Claus (and thanks to Santa's friend, Phyllis, for sending this review along!)

*"My nose isn't the only thing glowing after reading Holly's **Spruced Up**, so is this review! A glowing review… get it?? (I've found people humor is very different from the reindeer games I'm used to, so I wanted to be sure you understood that was funny.) Anyway, the story shined… or shone… or… I'm just a reindeer, so I'm not sure about the grammar, but let's just say, **Spruced Up** was holiday fun!"* ~Rudolph, The Red-Nosed Reindeer

"Not a big mystery, but an awful lot of Christmas spirit… a touching story." ~Ebenezer Scrooge (Holly said this should be a funny review but even though I discovered my Christmas spirit, I still don't have much of a funny bone.)

TABLE OF CONTENTS

Dear Reader,

I am a writer who likes to stick close to home, both in real life and in my books. But in the Maid in LA Mystery series, I moved the setting to Los Angeles and Hollywood. My friend Dee J. Adams has been very generous in making sure I stay pretty close to the facts. She patiently answered all my e-mails and stupid questions for the first book (*Steamed*) and second book (*Dusted*) in the series. Well, Dee, you're off the hook in this one because Quincy's coming home to Erie, PA for Christmas. This is a town I can speak about with authority. From our Presque Isle peninsula that juts out into Lake Erie, to the bayfront that sits at the foot of State Street and from the downtown area, to the Millcreek Mall area that sprawls along Peach Street. I grew up here. I love it here. I love setting most of my books here. And I'm thrilled to bring Quincy here.

Yes, Quincy's come home to the city by the bay...a city that is one of the snowiest cities in the US. (Look up the stats...we're there.) Now, after solving a murder, and then solving an art theft/forgery mystery, Quincy's ready for a vacation. But it seems that an article in the local paper has made her a mini-celebrity in her hometown. And some missing medical supplies throw another mystery in her lap...just in time for the holiday. This is a novella, but though the mystery is a small one, it's an important one in the Maid in LA series. It helps move Quincy's story arc forward.

For writers, characters can become real, and Quincy is that for me. So from Quincy, the entire Maid in LA Mystery gang, and from me as well: Merry Christmas, Happy Holidays, Happy Chanukah, Merry Kwanza, Season's Greetings, Super Solstice... basically, whatever holiday you're celebrating, I hope it's a lovely one that's filled with family, friends... and of course a lot of good books.

Thank you so much for making Quincy and her friends such a hit!

Holly

CHAPTER ONE

"**Q**UINCY MAC, YOU'VE done it," Lottie Webber screamed as I spotted her in the Erie International Airport. A giant Christmas tree stood in the corner of the lobby, holiday music played over the speakers, and people were dressed in winter-weather wear.

"Now where are your glasses?" she asked.

I was wearing my warmest coat, which in Erie could be considered a fall coat at best. I did own Uggs more as a fashion statement than winter wear. I'd had to dig to the back of my closet to find them when I packed.

I took in the sights and sounds...I was home.

Before that feeling truly set in, I was swept into my childhood best friend's hug—which was well padded by her down coat. Gone were the two career women we'd grown into. As we hugged, we were both squealing like we were high school girls again.

Yeah, it's not pretty when two women pushing forty act like they're fourteen, but sometimes it can't be helped. It had been years since I'd seen Lottie but she hadn't changed at all. Lottie was short and twiggishly built. With anyone else who was so darned cute, I'd have been tempted to suck in my stomach, but this was Lottie. I knew she loved me baby-pooch and all.

"I didn't know that maids get red carpet treatment," I said when our squealing abated. "But I still have my glasses."

I was pleased I'd thought of those star glasses. Lottie had given them to me so many years ago when I left Erie, Pennsylvania for Hollywood, California. I'd had my bags, my glasses, and dreams of stardom.

I might not be a star, but I'd built a good life in LA.

Still I pulled out the glasses and slipped them on.

Lottie squealed all over again. "Really, you kept them? All these years?"

"Of course I did. Sorry I didn't ever get to wear them on a red carpet. They don't give awards for an almost toothpaste spokesperson. I missed the fame and fortune boat."

"Are you kidding?" Lottie reached in her gigantic purse—I mean, my carry-on that held an entire week's worth of clothes was only slightly bigger than her purse— and pulled out a copy of The Erie Times-News, our local newspaper. "It was in the paper."

There I was. My Name. Above the fold. Yes, I'd made the front page ... of the Local Section.

Erie's Own Quincy Mac Cleans up Crime in Los Angeles

I read the paper's online version, GoErie.com, most mornings. I like to keep up with what was going on back home. But between packing for myself, and for the boys, who were spending the holiday with their father and Peri, and then the flight across the country, I hadn't read the paper in a couple days.

I skimmed the article.

Move over Sherlock Holmes. Erie's got its own super-sleuth, Quincy Mac. Mac is an Erie native. She's the daughter of two local, prominent physicians. But rather than following in their footsteps, like her brothers, she moved to Los Angeles. She did some acting. Most recently she's the owner of a successful business. But cleaning up other people's homes wasn't enough for this intrepid entrepreneur. In her spare time, this maid in LA has solved not only a murder, but also an art heist. ...

"Isn't that awesome, Quincy?" Lottie said, her voice still near squeal pitch. "Look, there's your picture."

My picture was below the fold. And where on earth had the paper found it? It was an old headshot. I had a toothy grin in it. My agent at the time told me that smile had convinced the Dazzling Smile's execs I should be their commercial's star. Maybe that would have made my career. If only they hadn't found arsenic in the toothpaste.

"You have to sign it for me, Quince," Lottie said.

"Pardon?" I was still marveling at being compared to Sherlock Holmes.

"I need you to sign my copy of the paper. You might not be a movie star, but they said you're writing a screenplay based on the murder you solved? You hold onto those glasses you might need them yet."

She thrust the newspaper and a red Sharpie marker at me then she squealed again.

Everyone turned to look at us. Lottie pointed at me. "She's famous. This is Quincy Mac, Erie's own Sherlock Holmes, according to the Erie Times-News. She's a Hollywood screenwriter."

"I'm a Hollywood maid," I said loudly.

"You're a Hollywood business owner—a successful business owner." She stood there, paper and marker extended. I put down my bag and signed away. A big, flourishing *Quincy Mac, Maid in LA.*

Lottie had always believed in me. When I said I was going to Hollywood to become an actress, she fully expected to see me walking down a red carpet someday. She didn't seem to realize that I'd never actually done that.

Lottie and I had been friends since my first day of kindergarten. She was one of the most big-hearted people I'd ever met. I've seen her give crayons and pencils to schoolmates. I've watched her go buy a drink and sandwich for a homeless person. And once, a chipmunk ran out in front of her car. She thought she'd run it over and started to cry. We had to turn around in a driveway and go back to check. Thank goodness it was a fast chipmunk. I don't think she could have handled it if she'd smooshed it.

That was Lottie—all heart. The fact that she'd become a nurse was no surprise to anyone who knew her.

Standing in the middle of Erie's airport, wearing star glasses and signing a newspaper article, I knew without a doubt that I was famous to her. She'd always see me as a star and never realize I was just a maid.

I handed her the now signed paper and marker, then took off the glasses and slipped them back in my purse.

"Are you ready to go?" I asked because people were still staring at us. An older lady in the back was actually pointing at me.

"Definitely. Your mom gave me the afternoon off since she was going to be in surgery and couldn't pick you up."

Lottie worked at my family's medical practice. Yes. Family. You see, my mother, father, two brothers and their wives were all doctors. My two sets of grandparents had also been doctors. The only people in our family who weren't doctors were me and my Uncle Bill. Uncle Bill spent two years in jail. Now, I should mention he went to jail for a crime he didn't commit but it was a horrible scandal in the family. Not only was he an ex-con, he had a tattoo.

If I'd come to town in the spring and my mother had sent Lottie, I'd have chalked it up to Mom being embarrassed of me and sending her minions to do her bidding. But the last few months, things had changed with my mom. She didn't harp about my wasting my talent by not becoming a doctor. She actually seemed impressed that I'd found both a killer and an art thief. To be honest, she was actually over-the-moon excited by the idea of my screenplay.

Frankly, I think she had a bit of a crush on my writing mentor, Dick Macy. (Yes, really, rather than use any of the other nicknames for Richard Macy, he went with Dick. Dick Macy. Geesh.)

Lottie and I slogged through the snowy parking lot to her four-wheel drive SUV. Erie, Pennsylvania was known for a few things. Its proximity to the Great Lake and Presque Isle peninsula. The wonderful quality of life it provided its residents. Its low cost of living. Its scenic bayfront.

And it was known for snow. Lots and lots of snow.

Today's weather wasn't quite a blizzard, but there was a steady sheet of snow coming down.

"What's the weather say?" I asked. Weather is a stereotypical conversation subject—one that indicates a lack of anything better to talk about. In Erie, especially in the winter, weather is one of the best things to talk about. If you don't like the weather at that moment…wait an hour and it would change.

"Definitely a white Christmas," she assured me.

I resisted the urge to clap. I'd lived in LA for my entire adult life and missed white Christmases.

It was going to be a great holiday.

CHAPTER TWO

THE HOLIDAY WAS GOING TO SUCK.

After a lovely lunch with Lottie and some catching up (she has two high school girls, a deadbeat ex, works at my parents' practice, and volunteers at a local health clinic) she took me to my family's office. It was The Mac Practice. I tried coining the nickname Mac-Prac. It never caught on.

My mother was at her desk and smiled as I walked into her office.

"I'm so excited about spending the week with you, Mom," I said, meaning it. "Dick is hoping I can make a last pass on editing this script, and I could use some time to relax." Between murders, stolen forged paintings, Tiny's wedding, the boys, and a new boyfriend, it had been a busy few months. I had fantasies about this week. Things like sleeping in, late breakfasts, and maybe a frivolous day at the Millcreek Mall and all the other stores on Peach Street, Erie's shopping mecca.

"About that," Mom said slowly in a tone I recognized— that tone stopped my relaxing-week thoughts in their tracks. That particular tone had never boded well for my plans. That tone assured me the holiday wasn't going to be what I'd planned.

"I was hoping you'd find a little time to help me out."

"Sure, if I can." I thought adding the *if-I-can* caveat was wise. My mom is a tricky woman. "You know if *I can* do something, I'm willing to help, Mom. But I'm only here until Christmas."

I was flying out first thing the day after Christmas. Jerome and Peri would be dropping the boys off that day at dinner. Cal, my newish cop boyfriend, Tiny and her new husband Sal would come over, too. It was my day-after-Christmas Christmas dinner. Since I'd be flying that day I couldn't cook... I was having the meal catered by my friend Honey's restaurant.

Darn. No cooking. I'd have to just curl up by the tree and enjoy the day.

My mother stood up and walked toward a door in her office. "Come with me. I have a surprise."

She opened a door in her office that didn't lead into the hall. I knew that it didn't because I'd just come in from the hall door and this wasn't that. This door led into a small windowless room. Even with no windows, Mom didn't need to flip on the light in order for me to see the giant white-board that was the room's focal point.

When she did turn on the lights, I could see that this cubby had been made for viewing x-rays and for storage.

The x-rays didn't interest me in the least, nor did the boxes, files and books that were on the shelves. The white-board in the center of this glorified closet held my attention like a dog's eyes trained on a bone.

I knew why I used white-boards, but I couldn't figure out why my mother would want me to use this one.

"I have a little mystery I'd like your help solving," Mom said.

If this were a movie (I'm working on that screenplay and have movies on the brain), they'd cue the ominous *da da da dum* music here. This wasn't a movie, so the only sound was me saying, "Um." That was as noncommittal as I could manage.

Now, when you want to impress a highly respected surgeon who is invited all over the country to speak and has had numerous papers published—which in medical and academic circles is the thing to do—having *um* be your go-to response is not recommended, at least not by me. So I tried to add a bit of oomph to it by saying, "Mom, you do know I'm not a detective?"

The question was more of a stalling tactic than anything. My mother was very well aware of the fact I wasn't a detective.

"Quincy, I won't have you belittling your talent. Since August you've solved a major theft and forgery case and a murder. I am so proud of how you used logic and tenacity to find the culprits in both cases. This is just a minor case of some missing office supplies. Well, not just some. Actually, as far as we can tell, there have been a significant number of supplies that can't be accounted for. Everything from gauze, to tongue depressors, to blood pressure cuffs. It's not just the money, though no one likes losing money. It's the thought that someone we have working for us—someone we trust and consider part of our family—is stealing from us."

Now, I can understand stealing major works of art and replacing them with forgeries. The money was good and it seemed like a victimless crime. But medical supplies?

"How did you find out?" I asked.

"We were looking over invoices and noticed we seemed to be buying more supplies than in the past. More supplies than we thought we used. So your father and I did an inventory. We went back and looked at our records. It seems we've had supplies stolen for a long time. It's added up to quite a lot of money."

"Is someone involved with one of those international medical aid things? Maybe they took them to send overseas?"

"No. We'd hear about it if they were. Your brother, Gil, is the one who approves our charitable donations. You can check with him, but no, I haven't heard about anyone asking for help."

Well, it seemed to me if they were stealing supplies, they weren't asking. But maybe they'd asked and Gil had said no.

"Your father and I, well, we haven't said anything to anyone about this," my mother said. "Not even your brothers. It's just that..." She paused and my mother, who was the queen of not showing her emotions, actually looked broken up.

"Quincy, we think of everyone working here as family. When we all decided to start our own practice, that was why... the chance to work with family. And every nurse, receptionist, or clerk we've hired has been someone we felt would enhance that feeling. When a patient comes to see us, we want them to feel as if they're part of our family, too. The thought that someone we trust stole from us. Well, it hurts. Your father and I want to find out who and find out why. There may be a logical explanation."

I could see how much the idea of someone stealing from the practice hurt my mom. Not too long ago, I'd have stood there awkwardly, not knowing how to handle my mother's pain. But now I reached out and hugged her.

My mother hugged me back.

It was a moment.

And despite the fact I'd planned to come home and just relax, visit, and write for a week, I found myself saying, "I'll look into it, Mom."

As if he had some psychic connection, moments later Dick called.

"Are you writing?" was his greeting. "Because as soon as you come home my agent wants to meet with you."

"I promise, I will. But I might have a bit of a mystery to solve first."

I swear, Dick's squeal of glee outdid anything Lottie and I had managed. It pierced my eardrum.

"Do tell," he commanded.

And even though some missing supplies didn't rise to the level of a murder or stolen art, the fact that it mattered to my mother—that my mother had asked me to find out— meant that solving this mystery meant a lot to me.

I was only here for a week, so I had to get to work.

CHAPTER THREE

I GOT UP THE NEXT MORNING, waved everyone off and curled up with the newspaper. Normally if I want hometown news I use GoErie.com and read the paper on my iPad. But there's something about reading the real paper that is so much better.

I love shaking it out, working to get it to hang just right. I even love starting an article and then flipping through the section to find the ending, then flipping back to start another piece. And I really love doing all this with a cup of coffee next to me.

My parents' house was on the west side of town. We used to live up in Frontier Park, but when I was in my teens, they'd bought the house on Lakeshore Drive. It was too cold to go out on the deck, but I sat in an armchair near the northern window and watched the bay. It was grey today, reflecting the grey clouds and sky overhead. I'd even lit the gas fireplace and plugged in the Christmas tree lights.

My mother had gone all out this year. Her common denominator was buffalo plaid. That black and red check was mom's favorite. She'd found Christmas tree skirts and branches shaped into stars with plaid bows. She'd put up red LED lights on the tree. It looked beautiful and rustic.

The house was utterly quiet and smelled like the spruce tree.

I missed the boys, but there was something to be said about my morning of quiet. I lazily read the paper in between staring at the bay and alternately staring at the tree.

Really, the quiet was—

As if on cue, my cellphone rang. I might have been annoyed, but Cal's picture flashed on the screen.

It had been four months since Detective Caleb Parker tried to put me in jail for a crime I didn't commit. A crime I'd merely cleaned. It had been a little less than those four months since we'd been officially dating.

And only a couple months since he'd first said he loved me.

I said I loved him back.

I had thought that by now that first rush of infatuation would have faded, but it hadn't. I felt warm with it as I picked up the phone and said, "Hi."

I know, brilliant opening right?

"Hi," he said, echoing my salutation. "How're things in Erie?"

"I think what you're asking is how am I getting along with my family."

He laughed. "Yes."

"Fine. We're having a family dinner tonight."

"Your mom's cooking?"

"I certainly hope not. But she did make the reservations."

He laughed. "How about Christmas dinner?"

"Wegman's is delivering that. Domestic-ness is not her thing. I've given it some thought and I think the fact I'm a maid might be a form of rebellion."

He laughed again. We went on and talked about … well, about not much of anything. Since I solved two mysteries, he's hesitant to even mention cases he's working on. He's afraid I'll run out and try to solve all the murders in LA.

I keep trying to assure him the only reason I felt the need to solve my first murder, then the art heist, had to do with being selfish. I didn't want to go to jail or lose my business.

I wasn't sure he totally believed me. But I was okay with not talking about murder on a daily basis. So I didn't press him. Frankly, I figured since he spent all day solving homicides, talking about anything else had to be a welcome break.

So we talked about him having dinner at Big G's, and how Tiny and her new husband were doing. He asked about the boys, who were spending the week with their father and his newest wife, Peri. They'd all gone to New Zealand. Jerome was producing a new movie and wanted to scope out the setting.

My middle son, Miles, was beyond ecstatic. Jerome had promised to take him to the Weta Workshop. I wasn't sure what a Weta was (seriously, say that five times fast), or why they needed a workshop for it but I didn't ask because I knew Miles would be disappointed in me. I planned on Googling it before their next call.

As our conversation wound down, Cal said, "I've got to go. I've got a murder to solve."

"Me, too. Well, not the murder—"

He interrupted. "I definitely hope not. Quince you promised and I—"

I interrupted back. "Not a murder but a mystery. Some supplies are missing at my parents' office. Well, not some, but quite a few. Enough that they noticed. They don't want to make any accusations without facts, so Mom asked me to poke around."

I could hear Cal's sigh of relief. "A doctor's office missing supplies sort of case should be safe enough."

"And Dick is thrilled I've got a third mystery for my new franchise." Dick was sure I was going to be LA's next hot screenwriter. He was convinced I could turn my first Maid in LA mystery, which he'd titled Steamed, into a first movie in my own series.

Cal laughed. "I'll talk to you tonight if I can."

"Have a good one." There was a long pause, and then in perfect synchronization we both said, "Love you."

I hung up.

I'd been telling Cal I loved him for a few months and I did ... but it still felt odd to say. The last man I said *I-love-you* to was my ex. And while he was a fantastic father to the boys, I'm not sure I ever really loved him. And I'm absolutely positive he never really loved me. He was—and is—a serial monogamist. Every four or five years, he marries, divorces, then repeats the process. His current wife, Peri, was my favorite. We'd become close and she'd confessed that things with Jerome were feeling off.

As I headed to my parent's office, I worried about Peri and how she'd handle it when Jerome told her it was over.

As I drove, I realized that Erie had changed a lot since Lottie and I were kids. The new Bayfront Highway was a prime example. It shot along the bay, connecting Erie's east and west sides, as well as our two major interstates, I-90 and I-79. I wasn't prepared for how fast it dumped me at the office.

When my family all decided to go into practice together, they'd moved into the fourth floor of the new Perry Building at the foot of State Street. It looked out over the bay and had one of the local hospitals right across the street.

"Quincy," Lottie screamed as I walked into the office. "Hey, everyone. Quincy's here. Quincy, I think you know everyone except for maybe Jocelyn. She's new. Oh, and Carson. He's new, too. Guys, this is Quincy Mac. The famous detective and soon to be famous screenwriter, Quincy Mac."

She pointed to a bulletin board in the reception area where the Erie Times-News article was pinned up.

"We're all so proud of you," she said. "So what brings you in today?"

"Oh, I'm just going to hang out in Mom's office until she gets back from the hospital."

Lottie gave me a funny look. Frankly on my annual visits to Erie, I rarely if ever visited my family's office, much less hung out there. But I just smiled and waved as I walked back to Mom's office. There, as promised, was a stack of printouts and files.

Now, I'm no accountant or medical supply expert, but it was easy to see the orders my mother highlighted were out of whack when I compared them to previous years'.

I looked at my mother's list of items she thought had been stolen. Gauze, bandages, antiseptics. No drugs of any kind. Mainly supplies. There were a few larger items that had been purchased and Mom couldn't place. A couple blood pressure cuffs (which as the relative of doctors I know is actually called a aneroid sphygmomanometer—it's a great Scrabble word), thermometers and stethoscopes.

Maybe some other doctor's office was sneaking in at night and raiding my parents' office?

That didn't make sense.

I made a list of employees' names. I put small checks by people who'd been with my parents' forever and were low on my list of suspects.

I had five names with no check. The two new people, Jocelyn and Carson. And three others I'd met or heard of but didn't know well enough to feel confident in their innocence.

Maybe that's not a scientific method of doing things. And I'm sure Cal would be quick to assure me it wasn't a police method either. But I was a maid ... and it worked for me. At least it gave me someplace to start.

I heard Mom's office door open, so I ran out of the cubby and shut the door behind me.

"Quincy, what's going on?" Lottie said, eyeing the door I'd just slammed.

Back in the day, I told Lottie everything. That inclination was still there. But I'd promised my mom not to say anything so I simply nodded at the door and said, "It's almost Christmas. No one should ever ask questions like that during the holidays."

She relaxed and nodded. "You're right. Want to go out tonight?"

"I'd love to, but there's a big family dinner tonight."

"Is your mom cooking?" Lottie's horrified expression said she remembered the times my mom tried to cook for us.

"No. We have reservations."

"Phew."

"Yeah, I know. How about tomorrow?"

"I've got the clinic. This time of year, it's crazier than normal. A lot of our patients don't have the best housing situations, and they certainly don't do preventive health measures."

"You spend a lot of time there." It was more of a statement than a question.

Lottie shrugged. "Since Newman and I divorced earlier in the year, I've had more free time. He takes the girls half the week and as much as they drive me crazy, the house seems too quiet without them. I'd rather keep busy doing something that mattered than moping at home."

"That's one of the things I remember most about you ... you have a big heart. You'll make it sound like you're volunteering to keep busy, but you and I both know that it's because you see people in need. You can't not help. That's what makes you … well, makes you you."

It was a convoluted sentence, but it was accurate. When we were little, Lottie found a baby robin and spent a week getting up every hour to feed it. She was and is all heart. When we were younger, she frequently led with her heart and left her head trying to catch up.

"I could meet you at the clinic, and we could go out from there."

"Oh, that won't be necessary. I'll call you Saturday. We'll figure out something."

"Sounds good. It will be like old times." Lottie and I used to spend any time we weren't together on the phone. "Do you remember how the boys used to complain we hogged the phone?"

"That never happens any more. Everyone has their own cell phone." She shook her head. "I think this type of reminiscing might be a sign that we're getting old."

We looked at each other and burst out laughing, then with the type of connection that only the oldest of friends have, said, "Never," together.

Chapter Four

"**S**O WHAT DID YOU FIND?" my mom asked as we drove up State Street and parked in front of Molly Branigan's Pub.

Rather than telling her I found squat, I asked, "What do you think about Mary Kay, Betty Lou, and Laurel? They're newish and I don't know any of them well."

"They've all be with us for. ..." She was quiet a moment as she thought, "probably five years. I like them all. They fit in well with the rest of the staff. They all were hired about the same time and they've all become good friends. Art calls them the *three amigos*. Gil just calls them *trouble*. I don't want you to think he means that in a bad way. He means it in pretty much the same way he meant it when he called you trouble."

If those three could give my very Mac-ish brother the same kind of trouble I gave him back in the day they were all right in my book.

"How about the two newest employees? Joslyn and Carson?"

"They've both fit in well. They're not exactly new. Joslyn's been with us a year and, oh, maybe a half. Carson a year."

"That means both of them were there long enough to have something to do with the missing supplies." I asked the question I didn't want to ask but knew I had to. "Are you sure they are missing supplies? Maybe someone made it look like supplies were stolen but in reality they were pocketing the money."

"I'm not sure how easy that would be. I think someone would notice when orders came in for less than we ordered."

"Someone did notice," I told her. "You and Dad did notice something wasn't right." Looking at the order forms and sheets, I figured someone could have made it look as if they were ordering more supplies than they were. But odds are, they'd have to have a partner at the suppliers'. And there was more than one supplier, so they'd have to have more than one partner.

No, I think that might get too complex. Simple was probably better, and more likely.

My mom shook her head. "I guess it is possible, but I don't think it's plausible. It would be hard for someone brand new to figure out how to make it work. They'd need a connection at each of the suppliers and. ...." She shook her head. "No, I don't think it's likely."

"Me either." It would have been easier for me. Money was a motive I could understand. Office supplies—I couldn't find a way to make stealing them seem worth it.

Mom and I walked into the lower eastside bar. Irish music blared over the speakers. Mom led the way and I followed her through the tight clusters of tables and patrons. Everyone was there already.

I looked at the table. My two brothers, Gil and Art, looked like younger clones of my father. Their wives, Tanya and Marie, respectively have always been nice to me, but I'll confess, I don't know them well. I see them when I come home for visits, but generally like this...in family situations. I looked at my mom and thought about how much our relationship had changed over the last few months. Maybe it was time to see about changing things with Tanya and Marie, too.

"Quincy," they all said. It was a rather staid welcome but given that it was my family where even understated excitement was overstated, I felt welcome.

"Hi, everyone." I sat on one side of my dad, and Mom sat on his other side.

I braced myself for a night of medical conversations and was practically shocked when Gil said, "So, about the forgeries?"

"Yes," Art said. "Tell us all about your new case."

And suddenly, everyone at the table was looking at me and waiting to hear what I had to say.

It was an unusual experience.

No one in my family has ever asked me about removing a stain or the proper way to polish silver.

It felt nice.

I dove into the story. "It all started with a call from Theresa—"

My mom filled in, "The worst employee that Quincy's ever had."

"Yes," I said, then finished the story, most of which had been covered in the paper. Still, they sat through dinner, listening to my version, and asking the occasional question.

The conversation eventually made it to medicine, but I didn't mind. I'm probably the only LA maid who knows what ankylosing spondylitis is. (Chronic inflammation of the spine and sacroiliac joints.)

It was actually a very nice family diner.

On Friday I went into Mac-Prac (see, it sort of rolls off the tongue, doesn't it?) at lunchtime. Mom and Dad had put in a very nice lunchroom with a full kitchen at the new offices. On Fridays, they have lunch brought in and the office eats in shifts.

I wanted a chance to get to see the new employees up close without being obvious. Although, having the bosses' daughter/sister/sister-in-law hanging out in the break room wasn't ideal, it was the best I could come up with.

I made cookies that morning and brought them in warm. "My family feel like you all are family, too," I said. "Which makes you my family in a step-family sort of way," I said.

I'd have been less conspicuous if I'd come in to clean the place.

"So tell me about yourselves," I said to Betty Lou, Mary Kay, and Laurel. Mom had told me the three of them were hired about the same time and worked predominately for Art and Gil.

They all looked at me as if I were crazy. So I tried, "You know my brothers. They're not overly talkative. I remember, when we were little, we went on a car-trip from Erie to Boston. It was a good day's travel. Art read two books and Gil read one, though he argued how much they read should be measured by page-count, not by the quantity of books. His was some dusty tome on politics. Ask me what I read?"

Mary Kay obliged. "What did you read, Quincy?"

"Ten magazines. By the time we got to Boston, I was an expert on current fashion—though this was the nineties, so it wasn't great fashion by any stretch of the imagination. I also was well informed about everything that was going on in Hollywood."

They all smiled Laurel said, "My brother used to be infuriating he...."

All three of them talked about their siblings, about their families now, about my brothers. They laughed and ate, and they made me feel welcome.

For the life of me, I couldn't think of a subtle way of asking if they had by any chance purloined a significant quantity of supplies. But in my gut, I thought I knew the answer. No. They hadn't.

After they finished eating and went back to work, Carson and Jocelyn came in. They sat together as well. That made sense since they were a couple decades younger than the rest of the staff. I took cookies around to everyone, most of them I'd known for years.

I went to Carson and Jocelyn's table last. "Hi. You two are new here. I'm Quincy Mac—"

"Oh, Quincy, we know who you are. Your mom has gone on and on about her brilliant daughter, the super-sleuth, business owner, and mother extraordinaire. Have a seat," Jocelyn said. "It was nice of you to make cookies for everyone. But that doesn't surprise me. Your family is very nice. This is one of the best places I've ever worked. And I'm not just talking your mom's catered Friday lunches. It's the little things. My son had the flu a couple weeks after I started working here. I took him to my mom's, but when your mother heard I'd left him, she sent me home. She said, *When a child's sick, they want their mom. There are times you can't be there, but this isn't one of those times. Go. We'll all cover for you.* I heard she picked up a lot of the slack herself that day."

"I remember when I was little. I must have been in first or second grade. I got sick in school and Mom came to get me. I thought she'd take me to our babysitter's house, but she took me home and spent the afternoon making me tea and toast and watching Little House on the Prairie with me." Wow, that was a memory I hadn't pulled out in years.

There were other times I'd been sick and she'd had surgeries and had to leave me, but that day, she'd juggled her schedule to be with me. I kinda wanted to find her and hug her.

"Yeah, she's a special lady," I agreed. I needed to turn the conversation back to them. "What did you do before this?"

"I worked at the hospital but found I wanted something different. I knew your family from there, and when I heard they were hiring, I put my application in right away," Jocelyn said.

Carson had been quiet.

"And you?" I asked.

"Jocelyn told me how much she loved it here, so I applied." That wasn't the whole truth, I realized, watching the two of them sitting across the table. He'd followed her—and not because he'd heard how awesome it was here, but because he loved her.

I don't know what I expected, but I'd hoped interviewing the newer employees would give me some kind of clue. Something that would show me who did it. But the only mystery I'd solved was why Carson had come to work for my parents. He loved Jocelyn.

So, I made small talk with the two lovebirds and realized how much I missed Cal.

After lunch, I went back to my parents' house, plugged in the lights on the tree and called him.

"Hey, Detective, how's the new case?" I asked.

"Not talking about it," was his stubborn response.

I wanted to assure him I didn't need to figure out his case, that I was still working on mine and hadn't gotten anywhere.

So, I asked, "Any chance you'll be finished by Christmas?"

"Why?" He still sounded suspicious.

"Because I miss you and would love if you could take a couple days off." There. The truth was out. Seeing Jocelyn and Carson together had made me miss Cal.

"I'd like that," he said. "I'll see what I can do. How's your case?"

"I noticed you won't tell me anything about what you're doing, but you're quick to ask about what I'm doing."

He simply laughed. He was convinced I was a danger to myself after my two near death experiences—his opinion, not mine. I had everything handled in both cases. Anyway, he's positive I'm going to get myself killed with my new avocation.

I answered him, mainly to put his mind at rest. "I talked to all the new employees. They all seemed nice and genuine. I don't think they went to work for my family's practice because they're part of some international toilet paper fencing ring."

"Toilet paper?"

"Yeah, it's not just medical supplies. Orders are up across the board. Toilet paper, hand sanitizer … all of it."

"So what are you thinking?" he asked.

"Maybe someone's faking the orders and just pocketing the money. But the invoices seem legit. And if they did that, they'd either have to have an accomplice at each company we order from or they'd need to fake the invoices and our payments in a way that I haven't thought of. I've done our ordering for Mac'Cleaners, but I'm not a forensic supply invoice expert." I sighed. This was depressing. I found out who stole and forged the missing art, and I found out who killed Mr. Banning. Why was it so hard to figure out where these supplies went?

"Quincy, don't put too much pressure on yourself. You're supposed to be on vacation."

"Cal, my mom has faith that I can do it. She believes in me." And that was it in a nutshell. That was why this mattered so much. My mother was proud of my accomplishments, and she believed I could figure this out.

"Then take a step back," he said. "Go back to the basics. Ask yourself, what would someone's motive be?"

"Thanks. I'll talk to you later."

"I love you," he said.

"I love you, too."

I sat in the warm glow of those words as well as the warm glow of the Christmas lights. I mulled over what he'd said.

Cal was right. Why would people take supplies?

To supply something.

Like?

Another doctor's office?

Or maybe to sell?

Money. We weren't talking high finance here, but from what I could glean, there were enough missing supplies to make someone a tidy little sum.

I'd start by looking at who worked somewhere else and maybe look at who had money problems.

My phone rang. I picked it up but didn't recognize the number. It was an LA area code though.

"Hello?" I said.

"Quincy Mac?" came a female voice I didn't recognize.

"Yes?"

"It's Nancy at your insurance agency."

"Hi, Nancy. Is something wrong?" The last time I'd contacted my insurance company it had been because Theresa dusted, dropped, and tore a client's painting. In the end it had been a forgery, along with a bunch of other clients' paintings. "Don't tell me Theresa had another accident."

Tiny and I kept saying we were going to have to fire her. Seriously, she was the worst maid we'd ever hired. If she had one more accident. ...

"No," Nancy said quickly. "I'm calling to deliver some very good news. There was a reward for finding the stolen paintings. The agency just confirmed you'll be getting the check."

"A reward?"

"You found out who stole a lot of art and filed fake insurance claims to boot." She named a figure that made my toes curl.

"Could you repeat that?" I asked weakly.

Yep. She said the same figure.

Wow.

CHAPTER FIVE

FRIDAY NIGHT, I decided that rather than trying to squeeze in some time with Lottie over the weekend, I'd surprise her. I'd head over to her clinic and invite her out to a late dinner if her ex had the kids or invite myself to her house if he didn't.

I had wine and snacks in my car in case.

The clinic she volunteered at was on Parade Street, the old main street of Erie. I'd always loved this street. Below Sixth Street it was mainly residential. I noticed the city had done some new bump outs and lighting. There was a sign that said, *Welcome to Erie's Historic East Bayfront.*

Above the residential area there was Erie's old business district. Kraus's Department Store had been there since I was a kid...and it had been there long before that. It had become an anchor to the street and really hadn't changed for as long as I could remember. It still had the wonderful array of...well, everything from cast iron pans, to lampshades, to housedresses.

The clinic was a few doors up from Kraus's. I parked on the street and walked into the bright waiting room that held about a dozen people.

I went up to the reception desk. "Hi, could you tell Lottie Webber that Quincy Mac will be in the waiting room waiting to take her to dinner?"

The woman jumped up, disappeared from view for a few moments, then the door into the back opened. "You're one of the Macs?"

I nodded.

She grabbed my hand and pumped it up and down. "I'm Molly and I'm so, so happy to meet you. Everyone will be. You come with me."

She led me down a hall to the last door on the left. "Come in. You can wait for Lottie here."

It was obviously the staff's break room. There were a couple tables, a comfortable looking couch, and a small kitchenette. There was also a tiny tree in the corner decorated with paper ornaments.

She saw me looking at it. "We ask our younger patients to decorate this tree and the one in the lobby.

"And look." She pointed to a bulletin board. There was a sheet of plaid paper. McLean plaid. I knew this because it was the plaid we used on Mac'Cleaner's logo.

There was white, bold lettering over the plaid. *A true physician treats the body, the mind, and the heart—they truly care for their community. They do not need proclaim their good works.*

Molly ran her finger over the paper. "I know your practice wants to keep everything quiet, but we put this up in honor of all the Macs have done for us. Whenever things look dire here, you all pull through and help. So, while none of us will ever mention all your donations, please know that we appreciate them. We'd have had to close our doors a dozen times over without your generous help."

"Molly, I'm not one of the Doctor Macs. I'm the other one. The maid."

"You're Lottie's friend from California." She paused a moment. "And so I broke your family's request that no one know about their generosity." She sighed. "My mother always said my mouth moves faster than a ducks ... butt. She was right."

I smiled. "Listen, I won't say anything if you don't."

She hugged me. "You might not be one of the doctors, but you've got that same kind of generous spirit.

"That's lovely of you to say," I told her. I patted her back and took a step back. "But my family ... they save lives and obviously support others who do the same. I just clean houses."

"Oh, no you don't. Lottie told us how humble you are. You also solve mysteries. You've raised three amazing boys, and ... well, Lottie loves you, so that means you are a person of quality. Lottie has discerning tastes."

She glanced at the clock. "Make yourself at home. I'll go check on the desk and Lottie."

I sat on the couch next to the tree. I noticed that all the construction paper ornaments had messages.

"*Thank you for fixing my throats.*" I wondered about the child who obviously had more than one throat.

Another read, "*I hate shots, but Miss Lottie does it quick.*"

"*Thanks for stopping Granpas coff.*"

I thought about pulling my laptop out of its bag, but I waited for Molly to come back with Lottie.

I didn't wait long. She burst through the door again. "Lottie's not scheduled today."

That's funny. I was sure she'd said she was. "Well, darn," I said rising. "I'll have to surprise her another day."

"Maybe you shouldn't mention you came and I gave up your family's secret. Lottie said they were very insistent."

"I won't."

Molly threw herself at me and hugged me. She had a kind of open heart that reminded me of Peri, and I felt a pang of homesickness.

"I'll try to come back with Lottie for the official tour. If not this visit, then the next."

"Just know that you come from an amazing family, Quincy," Molly said with a great deal of sincerity.

"I already knew that, but it's nice to hear."

I called Lottie as I walked back to my parent's office. "How about dinner?" I said by way of greeting.

"Sorry. I'm working at the clinic."

I stopped in my tracks. "You are?"

"I'm sorry I've been so busy Quincy. I'd love to get together, but I can't. Between work, volunteering, and the holidays. ..." She let the sentence fade.

I felt hurt, but I tried not to let it show in my voice. "Okay then. I'll see you at the office."

My oldest friend was avoiding me. She'd seemed so happy when she picked me up at the airport.

I went back to the Mac-Prac. It was only a few blocks. The receptionist was still there. I told her to lock up, and I'd let myself out when I was done.

I went back to Mom's office and let myself into the little cubby. I stared at the white-board. There were names of everyone who worked at the practice. Everyone but my family.

The newest people were in the center. After meeting them, I didn't really think any of them had done it. I knew I'd have to start looking at the older (older in terms of employment history not necessarily in terms of age) and that sort of broke my heart because I knew if one of them did it, my parents would be hurt.

For the next hour, I jotted notes for myself next to employee names. Then door to my mom's office opened, startling me.

"Mom?" I called.

"No, it's me."

I recognized the *it's-me* voice straight off and walked into the office itself. "Lottie. Hey, can you do dinner after all?"

"I know you know. You don't need to take me out to dinner in order to interrogate me."

Here's the thing, Dick keeps stressing I have to be careful when I write my script, *Steamed,* not to sound too *ditzy.* Yes, that's the word he used. Ditzy. And I don't think I am ditzy. I've managed to build a successful business with Tiny, and I've raised three great kids.

But here's the thing, when I'm writing about investigating Mr. Banning's murder, I'm trying to be honest. I was confused more than confident. And I was innocent and Cal assured me I wouldn't go to jail, I knew from experience that innocent people did go to jail. And years later, when they're exonerated, they still have to carry a tattoo and a memory of the experience with them, just like my Uncle Bill had.

So, despite what I knew, I had been truly afraid.

I don't think that made me ditzy... it made me shrewd.

But I didn't feel the least bit shrewd as I looked at Lottie and tried to decide what she knew I knew. Other than I wanted a chance to hang out with her and she was avoiding me, I didn't have a clue.

So I said, "Pardon?" which sounded more intelligent than *huh?*

Tears pooled in her eyes as she said, "Molly's never met a secret she can keep. She called me right after you left and told me that you'd been there and that she'd spilled the beans. I've seen the infamous white-board in here and I knew you were investigating for the practice. That's probably why you came home for Christmas."

"I came home to spend time with my fam—" I started.

Lottie interrupted. "I'd already planned on confessing. I just wanted time to find the money to pay them back. Here." She thrust a check at me. "I sold my car. That's where I was tonight. Well, I tentatively sold it. So don't cash that check until next week. The guy's supposed to bring me his check tomorrow."

I looked at the figure on the check and let out a long whistle.

"And here's my letter of resignation." She handed me an envelope. "I'm so sorry. I didn't set out to have something like this happen. The first time, I took a case of gauze. The clinic was out. I simply ordered a new case and paid for it to replace it. Soon I was taking more than I could pay for. I always made the donations in the practice's names. I told everyone that your family did their charitable giving in secret, and the people at the clinic accepted that. I felt so guilty. They always needed something, and I couldn't stop giving the supplies, so I took out a home equity loan to pay them back, but then my furnace blew and by the time I replaced it...."

She stopped. "Quincy, I don't have any excuse other than, I didn't mean for it to happen and I'm sorry. If your parents decide to press charges, I understand."

I didn't say anything because I didn't know what to say. I held Lottie's check and letter of resignation in my hand and let the implications of what she was telling me sink in.

Of all the people in the office, she was right there with my family on the *not-in-a-million-years* list.

"Quince, say something," she said as she cried. Not big showy wails but small hiccups of emotion that she couldn't contain. "Once I knew you were investigating, I knew you'd figure it out. I meant what I said, you're amazing."

"Lottie, I hadn't figured out anything. I'd have never suspected you."

"But—"

"Let me get this straight. You over-ordered and took supplies to the clinic on a regular basis."

"Not just regular, frequent. The fact that your family merged their practices means everything has been a bit disorderly. I do most of the ordering for everyone despite the fact it's more than one big practice, it's more like six small practices that coexist. I knew someone would figure it out eventually, and frankly, I think part of me wanted them to. I'm not cut out for a life of larceny. Why don't we go to your parents' now and I'll tell them everything."

"Stop." I handed her the check and the letter of resignation, my mind was whirling with possible ways of handling this.

"Here's what we're going to do. I'm going to write the check to pay my parents back and you're going to go talk to them tomorrow morning and explain what happened. And then you will hand them your letter of resignation." I didn't think they'd accept it, but she was right, she had to offer. As a business owner, I knew how betrayed the missing supplies made my parents feel. But after listening to Lottie's story, and having talked to Molly at the clinic, I knew if it were me, I'd forgive her. I suspected my parents would as well.

I realized how much of a godsend that call from the insurance agency had been. It would easily cover what Lottie had taken and have a lot left over. I thought about all the things I could do with that money. Apply it to my kids' education. Buy some shoes. Maybe a cruise.

But I wouldn't do any of that. "As for the clinic, and how it's going to survive without the donations, I have a solution for that, too."

Hey, who needs new shoes or a cruise? I was back in Erie, spending a holiday with my family, and I'd be heading back to California for a second holiday with more of my family.

I'd say I was a very rich woman.

"Quincy," Lottie said as she sobbed.

"It's Christmas, Lottie. It's a time for miracles, and it's a time when people should remember to be generous. It's going to work out."

And I knew that Dick was going to be disappointed because he'd never find out what happened with this case.

And although Lottie had to confess what she'd done to my parents, they'd never find out about my involvement.

I'd see to that.

CHAPTER SIX

"**I**'M SORRY." Lottie was crying as she told me about her meeting with my parents. "I handed them the check, and they wouldn't take it. They told me to donate the money to the clinic, and your mother said, *Lottie, next time just ask.* And then she told me that they'd try to set aside a certain amount for the clinic on a monthly basis. And then she said, *Whatever you do don't tell anyone.*"

Lottie's crying escalated. "You won't let me tell them, and she didn't want me to tell you. Your family is the most generous, amazing—" She was crying too hard to continue.

"Lottie," I said. Other than her name, I didn't know what else to say.

"Your. Mother. Said. Just." She hiccupped between a sob. "What. I. Told. The. Clinic. She. Said. Don't. Tell."

I hugged her and let her cry it out. Then I handed her the rest of my insurance reward. "Between this and my parents' help, the clinic should be solvent for a while. And whatever you do, don't tell them where the money came from."

I hadn't told anyone about the money, so no one would ever be the wiser.

Lottie gave me a funny look, then said, "I know you always felt your family wasn't proud of you and that you were the black sheep. But Quincy, you are a Mac to the core. Merry Christmas."

"Merry Christmas, Lottie." I wanted to tell her how much her belief in me had meant all those years ago as I got on the plane, heading to Hollywood with a dream and a pair of star-shaped glasses. I guess I was Mac-ish enough not to be able to put it together in words, so I simply hugged her again.

I think she knew.

Later that night my mother found me. "About the missing supplies..." she started.

"I'm sorry I couldn't find who did it. I know you believed in me," I said. "Let's remember that solving those first two mysteries was more accident than skill. Dick worries that I come off as ditzy in the script for *Steamed*, but I'm pushing to leave it the way I wrote it. I maintain it's more scared and confused with a comic twist than ditzy."

My mother frowned. I tried to tell myself I was rather used to disappointing her. I knew her pride over my investigating avocation couldn't last. "I'm sorry, Mom."

"Quincy, how long have you been friends with Lottie?" she asked.

"Practically all my life," I answered.

"I think she's proved to both of us something we've always known, that she follows her heart, even if it leads her down some sticky alleys. She told me."

I played dumb. "Told you what?"

And then my mother—my very Mac-ish mother—hugged me. "She told me everything. There are no black sheep in this family, Quincy Mac. I am so very proud of you."

And that was the best Christmas present I'd ever received.

EPILOGUE

THE NEXT MORNING, my entire family had gathered at my parents' house to unwrap gifts.

It was snowing outside. The fire was blazing. The tree was glowing. But that's not what made this Christmas so special. My family did. I looked at all of them and felt a sense of belonging that I'd never felt before.

The only fly in the ointment was they all kept looking at me ... well, weirdly.

They looked at me as if they were waiting for something. I wondered if my parents had a surprise planned. "So. ..."

My sentence faded on that one word as I realized everyone was looking toward the other side of the room. I could hear the sound of footsteps on my mother's hardwood staircase. I did a mental headcount and knew everyone was accounted for.

"Who ..." My sentence faded as first shoes, then legs, and finally Cal came into view.

Detective Caleb Parker.

My boyfriend.

"Merry Christmas, Quincy," he said.

"Merry Christmas," I echoed. I started to get up to run to him, but he shook his head.

"Quincy, I got in a while ago and went to your father first. I wanted to ask his permission to ..." He came over to me and knelt on one knee. He held out a Tiffany's box.

I may not have ever owned anything that came in a Tiffany's box, but most women over twenty recognize one when they see it.

I stared at it in my hand, then looked at Cal, who said, "Quincy Mac. Will you marry me?"

My family was all staring at me. Both Tanya and Marie were unabashedly crying. And if I wasn't mistaken, my mother brushed a tear from her eyes.

And Cal... Cal was waiting for my answer.

Part of me wanted to say *yes*.

I loved him. So yes seemed like it would be the appropriate answer.

But there was a part of me that worried it was too soon. I'd only known Cal since August when we'd met at Mr. Banning's murder scene.

That worried part of me remembered the last time someone swept me off my feet. That had been Jerome. I'd said yes to his proposal, went on to have what I thought was a happy marriage, and three boys. I put aside the dreams I'd taken with me to Hollywood. Then one day he'd divorced me.

"Can I see you in private?" I asked.

I saw a look of disappointment in his face, and it broke my heart. He got off his knee and followed me into my old room.

"I'm sorry," he said. "I thought it would be romantic. Your mom was excited and offered to help. I shouldn't have—"

I interrupted. "Cal, with me and you, there are no *shouldn't haves*. I love you and I know you love me. And that's why I know you'll understand when I say, I want to marry you. I want to be engaged to you. But not yet. I need...."

"It's okay, Quince. I get it."

"You don't. I came home and found Lottie waiting for me with an Erie Times-News in her hand. There was an article about me, about solving Mr. Banning's murder, and then the painting heist. Dick called. His agent wants to meet with me after the holidays. The boys are almost on their own and...."

I wasn't sure how to explain it to him when I hardly understood it myself. "I want to say yes. And I will say yes...but not yet. I left Erie with dreams and plans. I set them aside when I married Jerome and then had the boys. Those dreams got pushed further behind me when I started the business with Tiny. Finally, I have time to explore those dreams. All three of the boys will be away at school soon, and I want to try it on my own."

I shook my head and corrected myself. "Not on my own. I want you with me, but not...."

He kissed me. "Quincy, I get it. You love me, but you want time."

"I do. I love you so much, Cal. I couldn't stand it if you thought—"

He kissed me again. "I do know you love me, and I love you enough to give you that time. You can give me my ring back."

I looked at the Tiffany's box and shook my head. I mean, what woman in her right mind gives back something from Tiffany's? "I have a better idea."

He smiled. "You do?"

I walked over to my old jewelry box and pulled out a gold chain. I slipped the gorgeous ring onto it and hooked it around my neck. "If it's okay with you, I'll keep it and wear it here...we'll be pre-engaged."

"Pre-engaged?" He shook his head and smiled. "Only you."

"Hey, a pre-engagement has perks. Almost as many perks as an engagement, except I'm not planning a wedding, so I'm not insane." My friend Tiny had planned her wedding all through the summer and sanity had not been part of her planning. "I just want some time on my own...on my own with you beside me if that makes sense."

"Quincy, you can take all the time you need. I'm not going anywhere."

"Merry Christmas, Cal."

"Merry Christmas, Quince."

And then he kissed my Santa socks off.

Thank you for reading Spruced Up: A Maid in LA Holiday Novella! I hope you enjoyed it. If you did, please help other readers find this book by writing a review.

If you want to keep track of new Maid in LA Mystery releases (as well as my other books) you can sign up for my newsletter at HollyJacobs.com.

Check out Quincy's next adventure, Swept Up: A Maid in LA Mystery (#4)

Quincy's screenplay has been turned into a made (or maid?) for TV movie on the HeartMark Channel. She's swept up in Hollywood's glitz and glamour. After the Mortie Award ceremony, Quincy finds herself thrust in the middle of another life-and-death mystery.

Did you miss Quincy's first adventure,
Steamed: A Maid in LA Mystery?
Here's an excerpt:

When I moved to LA, I was an eighteen year old with stars in my eyes. Well, not exactly in my eyes, but rather *on* my eyes. My high school best friend bought me sunglasses with lenses shaped like stars for when I *Made It.* Lottie always said the words in such a way you just knew they were capitalized.

Made It.

Yes, I graduated from high school and moved to LA. I planned to be a famous actress. Lottie made me promise I'd wear my star-shaped glasses on my first Oscar red carpet walk. My goal was to take Hollywood by storm.

These days, those glasses are in a drawer in my bedroom and I have two much smaller goals. One is that I want to wear my jeans without a muffin-top. After three kids, I'd developed a bit of a baby-pooch that wants to creep out above the waistband of my jeans. I longed for the days when pants had waistbands that were higher. Back then you could tuck your baby-pooch in. These days your options are exercise, wear Spanx, or learn to suck it in.

I tend to suck it in … when I remember.

My second goal is an empty nest.

It's not that I don't love my boys. I do. I have three sons—Hunter, Miles and Eli. They are eighteen, seventeen and sixteen. I've been a parent practically my entire adult life. I'm ready for a time when I simply have to worry about me and no one else.

This summer is my trial empty-nest.

The boys left last night to spend four weeks in the Bahamas with their father and his most recent wife, Peri.

Now, my place isn't exactly a dump, but compared to their dad's house, my three bedroom bungalow in the out-of-the-way neighborhood of Van George is a cardboard box in some alley.

And while thirty-eight isn't exactly over-the-hill, next to Peri, the twenty-year-old, I am ancient.

I miss my boys (and I realize the irony in longing for an empty nest, but missing them when they're on vacation).

I try not to mind when my ex takes the boys on fabulous vacations—and most of the time I don't mind—but getting ready for work in a quiet house, I minded.

My ex, movie producer Jerome Smith, is a nice guy … a nice guy with a taste for younger women. Specifically women between the ages of twenty and twenty-five. The exact ages I married, then divorced him. Or rather, he divorced me.

Jerome had two marriages before me, and three marriages since, all within those same parameters. His current wife's my favorite. I really like Peri despite the way her breasts perk and mine just sort of … well, hang loosely if they're not strapped down. I think Peri sort of appeals to my maternal instincts. I don't have a daughter.

Maybe I'll adopt her when Jerome divorces her.

TGIF, I told myself. I'm thirty-eight, and until the boys come home from their summer visit with their father, I'm footloose and fancy-free.

Maybe it isn't exactly the life I'd dreamed of when I moved to LA, but it's a good life.

Oh, sometimes I still wish that I was starring in some movie of the week instead of heading into Mac'Cleaners.

Yes, that's right—I no longer have stars in or on my eyes. Rather than achieving stardom, I have three sons and clean houses for a living. It's honest work, and it's flexible enough that when I was younger I could take time off and go on auditions. Now that I'm part owner and thirty-eight, I don't go to many auditions.

Okay, so I haven't been on an audition in five years— I've discovered that I'm a size twelve girl in a size two world.

I missed the fame and fortune boat.

Okay, so I could live without fame or fortune, if only I could figure out what I wanted to do with my life sometime before menopause hit. Owning a business keeps the boys and me afloat financially but lately, I'd had a feeling that it was time for a change. The kids weren't such kids anymore. Hunter would start college in the fall.

That empty nest is just around the bend. Soon I'll be able to live my own life.

And I know I want something more.

I'd said I wanted to act since I was six. I never gave any thought to doing something else. But it's clear that acting isn't going to be my ultimate career.

So while I wait to figure out what I want to do, I clean houses. I need to figure out soon because I'll be turning forty in a couple years. Forty sounds so very grown up, and grown-ups should have some idea about the direction they want their lives to take.

But I wasn't going to think about direction today.

Today, I was going to get my work done and then go do something decadent.

I'd like to say I was planning to go to a bar and pick up guys—well at least pick up a guy—but I'll probably end up going to the store and picking up Ben and Jerry's, then head home and try and catch up on all the chick-flicks the boys make me miss.

Feeling a bit better, I walked into the small brick storefront that was only a mile from my house. It proudly proclaimed Mac'Cleaners on the plate glass window with a tartan weaving through the letters. I walked through the small reception room and back to my partner, Tiny's office.

Big mistake.

There's nothing worse than starting the day as a single, directionless, mother of three and then walking into the middle of the wonderful world of weddings.

Tiny's marrying Salvador Mardones in September. September 30th to be exact. And she's going slightly insane...a bit further over the brink each day.

"Tiny?" I called, hoping she was somewhere in the sea of tulle and satin.

"I'm here, Quincy," she said from the back corner.

Tiny's not very...tiny that is. She's five eight and looks like a model. Skin the color of strong tea and dark hair with a tendency to curl. She's gorgeous and simply a beautiful soul. We make an interesting pair, what with me having Irish fair skin, a light sprinkling of freckles that might have been cute when I was in my teens, but aren't as much when at thirty-eight. And my hair...well, it was blond when I moved to LA thanks to Lottie and Miss Clairol. These days, it has gone back to its brownish roots...literally.

Tiny smiled as I walked in, and I couldn't muster up true annoyance that her smile was messing with my grouchy mood because she radiated happiness. The kind of happiness I knew she deserved.

"It's getting worse, isn't it?" she asked, gesturing at her office.

I surveyed the room. "Yeah."

"I just can't help myself. I want this wedding to be perfect because Sal's perfect."

Truth is, Sal is perfect. He's my five five height, balding and has a beer belly that makes my small baby-pooched stomach look like washboard abs.

But he's truly one of the nicest guys in the world.

Tiny had a history of dating losers. But that was over because Sal...well, he's a winner.

"The wedding will be perfect," I promised.

I'd see to it, even though I'd rather have wisdom teeth pulled than plan a wedding this elegant.

Me, if I ever get married again, I'm eloping. Something fast and simple. Someone saying the official words, then me and my new husband back at some hotel having sex. Lots and lots of sex.

It had been a while, which might explain why my mind skipped right over finding Mr. Right and a wedding and went right to the sex.

"Speaking of help," Tiny said slowly, "we need some today. Theresa's out."

Rats.

"It's my turn, isn't it?" I asked, though I knew the answer.

She nodded.

When one of our employees calls in sick, we take turns filling in.

Today it was my turn to fill in.

I should have just gone back to bed this morning.

Grumbling to myself, I left Tiny to hold down the fort and took Theresa's folder for the day. The nice thing about working outside the office is that the day always went fast.

Today was no exception. By three in the afternoon, I was on my way to the last job.

As soon as I finished Mr. Banning's, I'd decided that I was going shopping for a new pair of shoes rather than Ben and Jerry's.

More money, less calories.

I thought the trade-off was worth it.

On a day like today, I didn't just want new shoes—I needed them. So, I grabbed Mr. Banning's printout from Theresa's folder. I was anxious to finish this last job.

Mr. Banning's was a BWP/wL.

A basic-weekly-pickup, with laundry.

I knocked on his door, even though the file said the odds of him being home at three o'clock in the afternoon were slim to nil.

I used our key and let myself in. I surveyed the living room with disgust. There was nothing basic about this job.

The place was a mess.

I mean, a real pigsty. Worse than my boys' rooms ... and that's saying something. Teenage boys are very toxic.

Mr. Banning was a whole new level of toxicity, though. Underwear was hanging from a chandelier, empty glasses and plates were scattered through the room.

Oh, geesh. Mr. Banning had a Mortie. All TV Network, ATVN, had begun to hand out the award ten years ago and it had quickly become one of the premier Hollywood awards.

Hey, I might not be an actual actress, but I know stuff.

I noticed not out of some sort of awe that I was cleaning a Mortie winner's home, but rather because the award was sitting in the middle of the leather couch, covered in something. Maybe someone had dipped it into some of the food. Ugh. It looked like they'd tried to wipe it off before throwing it on the couch, but they didn't wipe hard enough.

To top it off, there were footprints on the light beige carpet. Big footprints. Whoever wore those shoes had really big feet. Thankfully, there were only two. As if whoever made the prints realized they'd tracked in mud and took off their shoes, because those two prints were it.

Well, there'd been at least one considerate person.

I tried to make a mental list of how best to approach this job.

In the end, there was nothing to do but start. I gathered dishes and cups and the pots and pans in the kitchen and had the dishwasher running minutes later. I even hand-washed the Mortie—which was about as heavy as a bag of sugar, heavier than I'd thought the old-fashioned silver television would be—and gave it a thorough polish. When I was done, the inscription on the silver television screen really stood out. Steve Banning. *Dead Certain.*

I remembered that show. It was a comedy about a medical examiner's office.

I set the Mortie on the mantle, thinking that was a more appropriate place for it than the couch.

There was a desk next to the fireplace. It had an old relic of a computer on it. The keyboard's cord dangled over the edge of the desk. Yeah, that wasn't going to work well.

I plugged the keyboard into the back of the tower.

Next, I dragged a garbage can around the room and made short order of the rest of the mess.

I debated whether I should toss the chandelier's panties out, but opted to put them in the wash with a load of clothes. At least when Mr. Banning returned them to whoever they belonged to, they'd be clean.

Maybe they belonged to him?

The thought was enough to make me decide to concentrate on the job at hand rather than on the underclothing our Mortie-winning client wore.

There was a small steam-cleaner in the back of the Mac'Cleaners van. It made short work of the footprints. I worked on the laundry as I vacuumed and dusted. By then the dishwasher was finished, so I unloaded it then cleaned the kitchen.

I found the bra that matched the panties under the sink.

Personally, I didn't want to know why there was a bra under the sink. Maybe Mr. Banning had a dishwashing fetish and the mystery naked woman helped him out? The mental image was disturbing.

I knew walking into the place that Mr. Banning liked women.

It said so on his file. Right after BWP/wL it said *DOG*.

That's our code for he liked women a lot and liked a lot of them.

Yes, Mr. Banning is a dog…a letch.

But he never bothers the staff, so it didn't bother us.

Mac'Cleaners is an equal opportunity employee. We stake our reputation on good service and discretion.

This job was going to require a lot of discretion on my part. I wondered if Theresa's illness had anything to do with knowing that Mr. Banning's place was this bad and that she'd have to clean it up?

Kitchen done, I moved onto and finished the bathroom as well. Then I folded a load of laundry and put another one in the dryer. With the job almost done, I was getting excited about shoe shopping, which in LA is a unique treat. So many shoes, so few feet. I headed to Mr. Banning's bedroom.

If his living room was a pit, I really didn't want to know what condition his bedroom was in. Knowing that all that stood between me and some Santee Alley bargain shopping was this bedroom, I opened the door, took all of one step in and…screamed.

It wasn't a frustrated scream.

It wasn't even a this-guy-is-such-a-pig sort of scream.

No, it was more like a there's-a-bloody-dead-body-on-the-bed sort of scream.

Loud, long and more than a little crazed.

I wanted to keep screaming and run right out of the house, but I managed to get myself under control. The killer had to be long gone, or else he—or she—would have attacked me as I cleaned. I was safe. I couldn't say the same for poor Mr. Banning.

I reached in my back pocket, pulled out my cell phone and called 911.

"You've reached Los Angles emergency dispatch."

"I need help," I blurted out.

"What is the nature of your emergency?" the man on the other end of the phone asked.

"Mr. Banning's dead. There's blood on his head and his eyes are open."

Those eyes were going to give me nightmares for the rest of my life.

"Your address ma'am?"

"I'm at, he's at—" I had to think a moment, but then I somehow pulled his address from the fog that was my mind and blurted it out.

"Who are you?" the operator asked.

"I'm the maid. Quincy Mac."

Now, some people prefer the term domestic engineer, or some fancy title. I call it like I see it. I'm a maid.

I had no idea why I thought of what to call myself at that moment. Maybe it was nerves. After all it's not every day I find a dead client.

Thinking about my job description was easier than thinking about those eyes and all that blood.

"Ma'am are you sure he's dead?"

"I don't think there's any way someone could look that bloody and blue and still be breathing."

This was the ultimate topper to my day from hell.

A dead man in the bedroom.

As I talked to the operator, I walked outside. Not really walked, trotted. I moved fast. I mean, no way was I staying in a house with a dead guy.

. I was thankful for my cell phone as I stepped out onto the bright sidewalk.

Perfect.

All that LA sunshine made it hard to believe that someone was dead a short distance away.

The emergency operator continued asking me questions. The company's name, my name and address, etc...

Personally, I sort of zoned out. I think I answered him all right but couldn't be sure.

Actually, I didn't want to be sure.

I just wanted to go home.

The police arrived, followed by an ambulance. They stopped and talked to me a minute, then hurried off to check on Mr. Banning.

I wondered how long I had to wait around.

I wanted to go home now.

I mean, I didn't even want to hunt for the perfect pair of bargain shoes or stop for Ben and Jerry's. That just shows how hard I'd been hit by this.

Anytime a woman passes up Ben and Jerry's or new shoes... well, it's moved beyond a bad day and turned into a found-a-dead-body-on-the-bed sort of day.

I was wondering if I could just sneak out. The authorities had my information already, so they didn't need me. But then *He* walked up to me.

He was tall, lean and oh-so-yummy. Dark hair with just a touch of grey at the temples.

Not one of LA's boy-toys who are a dime a dozen.

No, this was a real man walking toward me like some hero out of a movie.

Maybe he was here to take me away from all this.

Maybe he'd seen me from across the street looking fragile, yet still beautiful.

Okay, so beautiful was a bit unattainable. I'd settle for fragile and cute. Yeah, I could pull off cute on a good day and I felt very, very fragile at the moment.

Ah, my hero.

I sucked in my baby-pooch, pulled out my old acting class skills and concentrated on looking even more fragile and cute. It worked. He walked right up to me, shot me a concerned look, then ... he flashed a badge.

I realized that his concerned look was more of an assessing look.

My hero was a cop.

Okay, so maybe *He* was a cop who was concerned because I looked so fragile?

"Ma'am? You're," he flipped open his little notepad in a very Adam-12 sort of way, and that particular mental-analogy really dated me I realized morosely as he finished, "Quincy Mac?"

"Yes." I thought about fluttering my eyelashes but decided to give up before I embarrassed myself.

"You're the one who found Mr. Banning and called 911?"

"Yes." I wanted to say more, so much more. But even a gorgeous knockout cop couldn't make me forget I'd just found a dead body, at least not for long. And thoughts of Mr. Banning, sitting on his bed, covered in blood with his eyes open, well, that sort of froze the words in my throat.

"The officer over there said that the house has been pretty much wiped clean."

I had professional pride in my job well done. "Not *pretty much*, all the way. Other than the bedroom, which I didn't clean for obvious reasons."

The cop quirked his eyebrow. "He said the bedroom was wiped clean as well."

I think the hunky cop just called me a liar.

Actually, I didn't just think it, I could see it in his eyes. The man actually thought I'd gone into a room with a dead body in it and cleaned it up?

My attraction to him slipped more than just a notch. It evaporated.

"Not by me," I assured him. "I took one look at the body on the bed, called 911 as I got the heck out of there. I guarantee that I didn't stop to clean the room first."

"But you admit you cleaned the rest of the house?" the cop asked.

"Of course I admit it. I'm the maid. That's what they pay me to do. Don't you think that if I'd have known someone had died, I'd have simply called the cops first? If you'd seen what a state the house was in when I arrived, you'd know I'd have welcomed an excuse not to clean it. But I did clean it and I did a fine job of it."

Cleaning houses is an honest profession. I might have been a bit befuddled, but even in my present state I wasn't going to let some cop make me feel less than the professional that I am.

He didn't answer my question. He simply asked, "And the other officers said there were footprints you steamed off the carpet?"

"Yes. I'm good at what I do. When Mac'Cleaners cleans a house, it's totally clean."

"Ma'am, the coroner says that Mr. Banning probably died sometime last night." He paused a moment and sort of gave me a hard stare with his charcoal grey eyes.

That stare did things to me...my knees felt rather weak and my heart rate sped up. I don't think it was shock.

Lust.

That's what it felt like.

I hadn't had a good case of lust in a while. But I was pretty sure that I remembered how if felt and this was it.

"Quincy," he said, soft and low.

Yes, I wanted to say.

Oh, yes.

I've read that when someone experiences death they want to make love just to prove they're still alive, to prove that they can still feel something.

I think my lust for this cop went deeper than just a need to prove I was alive. It might have been a need to prove I still had a libido, but mainly I think it had something to do with a long, hard orgasm.

I was almost forty and I'd read enough magazine articles to know that meant I was reaching my sexual prime.

Only it had been a long time since I'd been primed.

This guy was making remember how much I enjoyed a good priming.

"Yes," I said out loud. Hoping he'd say, *let's forget about the dead body and get you home to bed.*

Oh, yeah. I wanted him to tuck me in, then tuck himself right next to me.

Naked.

"Quincy," he said again, "by any chance you have an alibi for last night?"

"An alibi?" I squeaked, all lust-filled thoughts fleeing from my head.

Alibi?

Rats.

I knew what that meant.

I watch *Law and Order, Law and Order SVU*, and *Law and Order Criminal Intent*. Is that all? I might be forgetting one, but that's understandable, given my circumstances.

Oh, and I watch *CSI*.

All that television meant I knew that cops didn't ask witnesses for alibis.

They asked suspects for them.

I was a murder suspect.

Check out Book #1 **Steamed: A Maid in LA Mystery**

Quincy Mac is a maid in LA—a maid who's accidently cleaned a murder scene. Now she's a murder suspect with only one option— find the real murderer before she ends up in jail for a crime she didn't commit. Quincy came to LA looking for fame and fortune. What she's found is infamy and misfortune. There's a killer out there, and Quincy's going to them… or die trying.

Did you miss Quincy's second book, **Dusted: A Maid in LA Mystery?** *Here's an excerpt:*

I looked in the mirror and felt nothing but… horror.

Orange?

I have never owned any orange clothes, so I must have suspected all along that orange might not be my color, but looking in the mirror, I was positive—orange was soooo not my color.

Frankly, I don't know that orange is anyone's color. I mean, Tiny could keep calling it *rustic pumpkin* until the cows came home, but the fact of the matter was, my maid-of-honor dress was orange.

The other fact of the matter was, I looked like giant pumpkin.

"Quincy Mac, you are absolutely stunning." Tiny's voice was all breathless wonder.

The last two weeks she'd gone from wedding-itis to full blown wedding-fever. Everything she said was breathless.

Breathless wonder.

Breathless excitement.

Breathless anticipation.

"Breathe, Tiny," I reminded helpfully as I had countless times the last few weeks.

"You look so…" She stared to cry.

Breathless and crying. Those were Tiny's two modes of communication as her wedding day drew nearer.

I filled in the blank while I waited for her to compose herself.

You look so… *much like a pumpkin.*

You look so… *scary.*

You look so… *much like a tangerine.* Oh, who was I kidding, I was no tiny tangerine. I was a full-on navel orange.

I sucked in my baby-pooch and wished I'd thought to bring my body-sucker. Oh, I know that's not what it's actually called. These days people call them by their name brand. My Grandma Mac called hers a girdle and I don't think I ever saw her without it on. I'm pretty sure she was buried in it.

Note to my boys who would some day be in charge of burying me. Do not bury me in a body sucker.

"…so beautiful," Tiny finally managed.

I smiled and put all of Mr. Magee's acting classes to use by assuring her, "I love it, Tiny."

I didn't love it, but she did and that's all that mattered. Too many people forget that a wedding is the bride and groom's special day. It's the one day when thinking about yourself isn't the least bit selfish. If she wanted me to look like a pumpkin, then by gosh, I'd be a smiling pumpkin as I walked up that aisle.

Tiny's wedding was three weeks away. I had promised myself I'd do everything in my power to be sure it was perfect.

Heck, I'd even found out who murdered Mr. Banning in order to see to it I wasn't in jail for Tiny's wedding.

Okay, truth was, I didn't want to be in jail period. And since I'd accidently cleaned Mr. Banning's murder scene, I was the only viable suspect.

Yeah, that's right. I cleaned it. I washed and polished the murder weapon. I even steamed the footprints off the carpet.

My Uncle Bill went to jail for a crime he didn't commit. Eventually the authorities realized he was innocent. They let him out of prison, but he came out with a tattoo. Mac's do not get tattoos. Or go to prison for that matter.

I was determined not to go to jail and leave my boys, or miss Tiny's wedding... or get a tattoo. I just didn't think a tattoo would age well. I was thirty-eight, and though I avoided the sun as if I were a vampire rather than simply a fair-skinned woman, I knew that wrinkles would be forthcoming. And who wants to see a wrinkled tattoo unicorn, even if it was a declaration of my innocence?

No one, that's who.

Thankfully, I found the murderer. Of course, he tried to kill me to keep me quiet, but I grew up with brothers and three sons. I kicked him and made it count. I rescued myself before Cal came in to rescue me.

Detective Cal Parker, my new boyfriend. It felt so odd to use the word *boyfriend* when I was the mother of three teens and almost forty (sigh) but I hadn't come up with any better designation for him.

I must have sighed as I thought about my cute, hunky new boyfriend because Tiny laughed. "You're thinking about him, aren't you?"

"Him, who?" I asked, trying to sound as if I didn't have a clue what she was talking about.

"Him—Detective Sexy."

"I was thinking about your wedding."

Tiny laughed some more and humphed me in a way that I knew meant she wasn't buying it.

The phone rang. I sucked in my stomach as I walked across the room in my pumpkin colored dress. I picked up the phone. "Mac'Cleaners. We do it all and we're glad you called. How may I help you today?"

"Quincy, it's me," a woman's voice said.

I didn't need any more than that to know it was Theresa Maxwell. She was officially the worst employee Mac'Cleaners had ever had. To be honest, that whole cleaning-Mr.-Banning's-murder scene was her fault because she was supposed to be the one cleaning the dead-body house that day, but she'd called in sick. When an employee calls in sick, Tiny and I—as the business owners—step in and fill in for them. So Theresa is why I'd almost ended up in jail for a murder I didn't commit.

Theresa really was the worst employee ever, not just in an almost-sent-me-to-jail sort of way.

I'd like to fire her. I'd threatened to do just that, but I kept hoping she'd get better. Seriously, she couldn't get any worse. Although this call didn't bode well for the getting better and seemed to be pointing to worse. There was panic in her voice.

"What's up, Theresa?" I asked suspiciously.

"It's not what's up, it's what's down. I was dusting a painting at the Gifford's house and it fell. There's a tear in it now."

I'd seen the Gifford's house when I cleaned for Theresa a month ago. The last call of the day had been the dead body house, but the Gifford's house was part of her morning calls, which became my morning call when Theresa called in sick.

I did not know much about art, but I knew enough to know their art was expensive. The Giffords lived in Hollywood Hills, an expensive part of town. I lived in Van George, where the cost of the houses sent my Pennsylvanian family into heart palpitations, but here in southern California was actually a mid-middle class sort of price.

"Oh…" I searched for a curse word I could use without being too crass or offending anyone. With three teenaged boys in the house, I really tried to watch myself.

"Boogers," I opted for. It was a pretty perfect curse word. Gross enough to get some umph out of, but not really offensive.

"I'm so sorry, Quincy," Theresa said. "I don't know what to do now."

"You'll have to call the Giffords and let them know what happened. Please take a picture of the damage with your cellphone, just to cross all our t's. I'll dot our i's by calling our insurance company to make a report. We've never had an accident like this happen, but please assure the Giffords we'll make it right."

"Okay," Theresa said and hung up.

I hit end on my phone and thumbed over to my contact list to look for our insurance company's number.

"Problems?" Tiny asked.

"Theresa," I managed.

"We're going to have to fire that girl," we said in sync.

I called the insurance company…

Check out Book #2 **Dusted: A Maid in LA Mystery**
Quincy's taking classes on writing and working on a script. She's taking care of her boys, wearing a pumpkin orange maid of honor dress for Tiny's wedding, and oh… she's got another case. Someone stole Mac'Cleaner clients' artwork, and Quincy's employee is under

suspicion. This is one LA maid who's got a lot on her plate in Holly Jacobs' second Maid in LA Mystery, Dusted.

Watch for Quincy's next adventure, Swept Up: A Maid in LA Mystery (4)

Quincy's screenplay has been turned into a made (or maid?) for TV movie on the HeartMark Channel and she's swept up in Hollywood's glitz and glamour. After the Mortie Award ceremony, Quincy finds herself thrust in the middle of another life-and-death mystery.

Bio

Award-winning author Holly Jacobs has almost three million books in print worldwide. The first novel in her Everything But... series, *Everything But a Groom*, was named one of 2008's Best Romances by Booklist, and her books have been honored with many other accolades. She lives in Erie, Pennsylvania, with her husband and four children and two dogs, Ethel Merman and Ella Fitzgerald. You can visit her at http://www.HollyJacobs.com.

ALSO BY HOLLY JACOBS:

Romance+ Stories
Just One Thing
Same Time Next Summer
Her Second-Chance Family
Words of the Heart Series
Carry Her Heart
These Three Words
Hold Her Heart

Romantic Comedies
I Waxed My Legs for This?
A Day Late and a Bride Short
Bosom Buddies
Cinderella Wore Tennis Shoes

Cupid Falls
Christmas in Cupid Falls
A Simple Heart: A Cupid Falls Novella

Short Stories and Novellas
Able to Love Again
Labor Day
There He Was
13 Weeks

Nothing But Short Story Series:
Nothing But Love
Nothing But Heart
Nothing But Luck
Rather than buy them individually, try:
Short Stories for the Overworked and Under-Read Anthology

Maid in LA Series:
My first mystery series!!
Steamed: A Maid in LA Mystery
Dusted: A Maid in LA Mystery
Spruced Up: A Maid in LA Novella
Swept Up: A Maid in LA Mystery
All four books in one edition
Maid in LA Mysteries bundle

Perry Square Series:
Do You Hear What I Hear?
A Day Late and a Bride Short
Dad Today, Groom Tomorrow
Be My Baby
Once Upon a Princess
Once Upon a Prince
Once Upon a King
Here With Me

Everything But ... Series:
Everything But a Groom
Everything But a Bride
Everything But a Wedding
Everything But a Christmas Eve
Everything But a Mother
Everything But a Dog

WLVH Series:
Pickup Lines
Lovehandles
Night Calls
Laugh Lines

Whedon Series:
Unexpected Gifts
A One-of-a-Kind Family
Homecoming Day
A Father's Name

Valley Ridge Series:
You Are Invited... *A Valley Ridge Wedding*
April Showers, *A Valley Ridge Wedding*
A Walk Down the Aisle, *A Valley Ridge Wedding*
A Valley Ridge Christmas